The GIRL
and the
DINOSAUR

For Sam, Nathan and Charlotte – H.H.

For Eve – S.M.

BLOOMSBURY CHILDREN'S BOOKS
Bloomsbury Publishing Plc
50 Bedford Square, London, WC1B 3DP, UK

BLOOMSBURY, BLOOMSBURY CHILDREN'S BOOKS and the Diana logo are
trademarks of Bloomsbury Publishing Plc

First published in Great Britain 2019 by Bloomsbury Publishing Plc

Text copyright © Hollie Hughes 2019
Illustrations copyright © Sarah Massini 2019

Hollie Hughes and Sarah Massini have asserted their rights under the Copyright,
Designs and Patents Act, 1988, to be identified as the Author and Illustrator of this work

A catalogue record for this book is available from the British Library

ISBN: 978 1 4088 8052 4

2 4 6 8 10 9 7 5 3 1

Printed and bound in China by C&C Offset Printing Co Ltd, Shenzhen, Guangdong

All papers used by Bloomsbury Publishing Plc are natural, recyclable products
from wood grown in well managed forests. The manufacturing
processes conform to the environmental regulations of the country of origin

To find out more about our authors and books
visit www.bloomsbury.com and sign up for our newsletters

The GIRL and the DINOSAUR

Hollie Hughes
and
Sarah Massini

BLOOMSBURY
CHILDREN'S BOOKS

LONDON   OXFORD   NEW YORK   NEW DELHI   SYDNEY

There's a town beside the sea,
not so very far from here,
with golden sands and rock pools,
and a tattered battered pier.

And there's a girl upon the beach,
her name is Marianne,
she's digging for a dinosaur
just beneath the sand.

Now, the fisherfolk all worry
for the girl beside the sea.
"She needs to find some *friends*," they say,
"and let those *old bones* be."

Still, Marianne is patient
and Marianne is clever,

and **stony bone**
by **stony bone** . . .

...a *beastie* comes together.

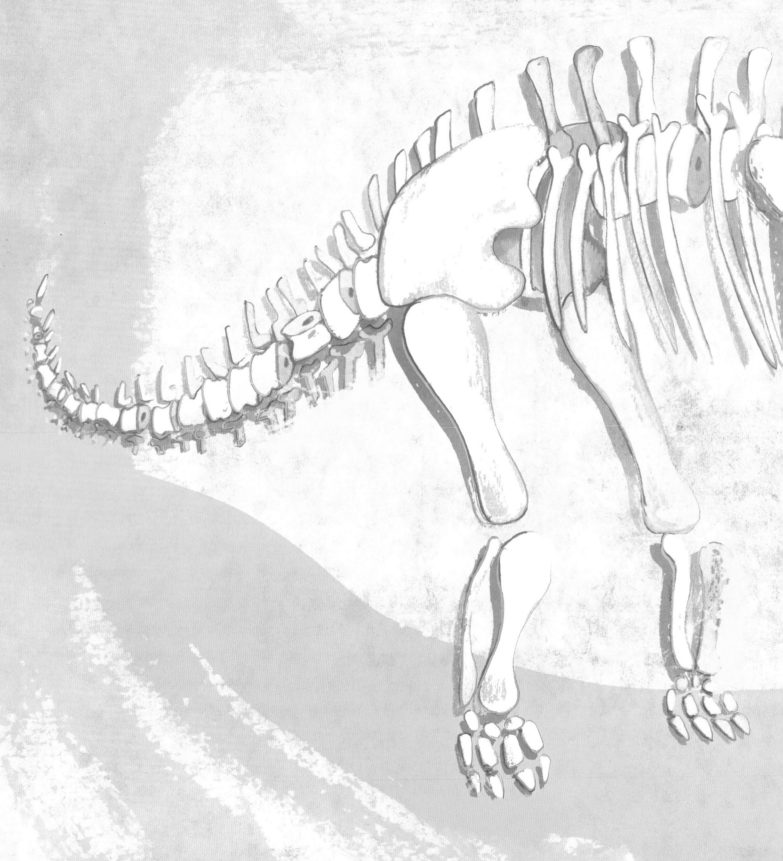

"I think I'll name you **Bony**,"
whispers little Marianne.
"And now that we are friends,
I'll be the **best** one that I can."

But the sleepy sun is setting
and Marianne must go.
"Sleep tight," she says to Bony,
"I'll be back before you know."

And when she climbs into her bed
and pulls the covers tight,
she offers up a *special wish*
into the starry night.

"With all my heart I make a wish,
and dream it will come true,
for stony bones to come to life
and find me when they do."

The wishing stars burn **bright** that night,
the air is thick with *dreams*,

and a deeply sleeping dinosaur
is waking up, it seems . . .

Then a *tap tap* at the window
– and Marianne's awake!
Her wishes have come *true*
and there are memories to make.

A bendy neck is offered
for a girl to slide right down,
and magic is now promised
in the sleepy starlit town.

Happily together, the friends go to the sea,
to bob with boats and fishes, their spirits wild and free.

Then onto new adventures
up a winding path of trees,
and they're flashing through a forest
like leaves upon the breeze.

Fairies float beside them
on their way to who knows what –
past *unicorns* and *giants*,
and creatures long forgot.

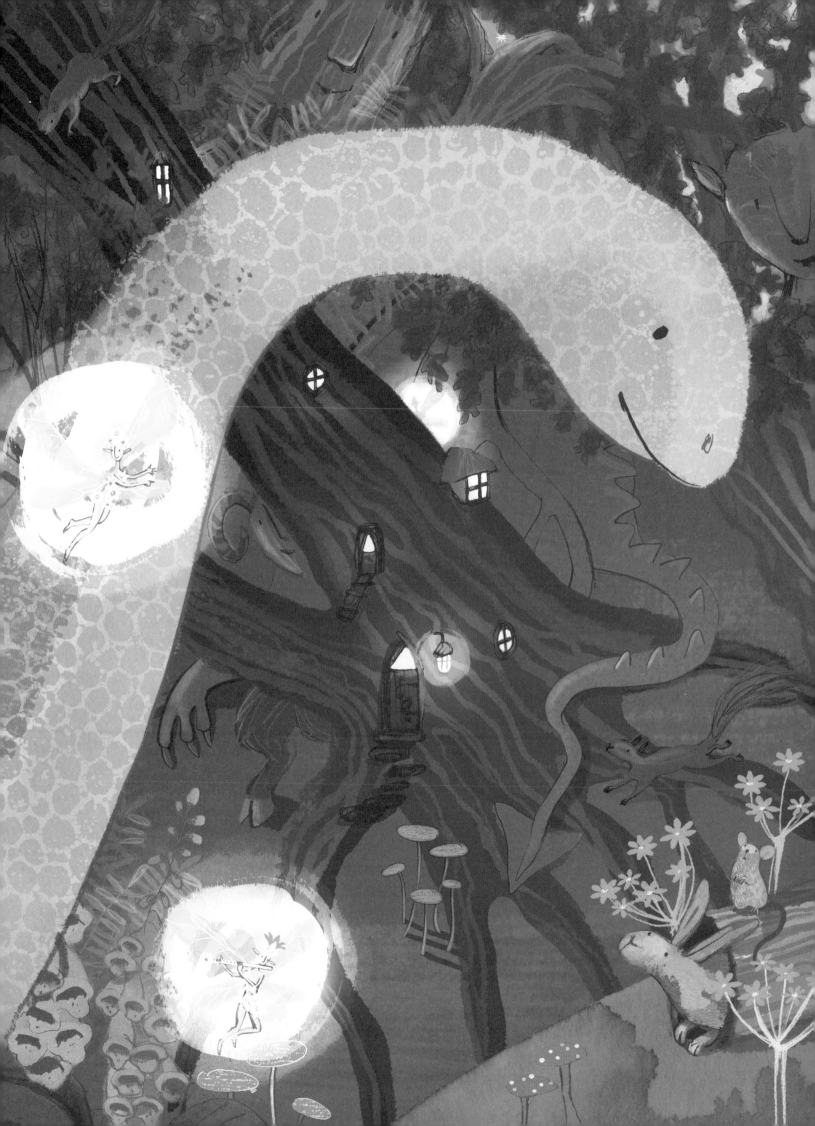

Up they climb, still higher,
hearts beating *boom-boom* fast,
till they reach a mountain summit
and stop for breath at last.

And, as the clouds all part,
they spy a land up in the sky –
a *magical* moonlit island
where night and daydreams fly.

With a mighty leap of faith, our brave dinosaur takes flight,
and then the pair are soaring through the dreamscape of the night.

Swooping,
gliding,
flying...

to the land up in the air . . .

And – *oh!* – what fun and magic
awaits the two friends there!

A **party** place for children and
the creatures from their dreams,
where *anything* is possible
and *nothing's* as it seems.

But slumber's pull is beckoning the children back to town . . .

It's time to leave the island
and begin the journey down.

Back to the town beside the sea
and back to empty beds,
and back to secret memories
to keep from grown-up heads.

And when Marianne snuggles down
and pulls her covers *tight*,
she slips into a dream-filled sleep
of *magic* in the night.

So, there's a town beside the sea,
not very far from here,
with golden sands and rock pools,
and a tattered battered pier.

And there are children on the beach,
with little Marianne,
each digging for their dinosaur
just beneath the sand.

The fisherfolk are happy now
and everything is well . . .

and as for *magic* in the night,
the children will not tell.